INTRODUCTION

High up above t[...] [...]
planet Earth is the [...] and [...] this
town is the little vil[...] [...]. Here you
will find a place cal[...] [...] Way, home to
some of the most int[...], amazing people you
will ever have the good fortune to meet - the Weather
People.

In the village lives Sally Sunshine, Theo Thunder, Lily
Lightning, Jack Frost, Clara, Clive and Claudia
Cloud, Harry Hurricane, Bobby Breeze, Rowena
Rain, Rosie Raindrop, Billy Wind, Darren Drizzle, Mr.
Moon, Shooting Star, Freddie Fog, Monica Mist,
Cedric Shower and many, many more.

So come with us, dear reader, and join us in some of
the many stories to be told.................

Chapter 1 - THEO THUNDER'S MAKEOVER

Hello reader. I think we all know someone who is permanently bad tempered and awkward. Sometimes they have had bad things happen in their lives which makes them pessimistic, very sad, or both. Or sometimes they just enjoy the mood. Theo Thunder was such a one. He usually ignored everyone around him but loved to argue for no reason at all (although he calls it debating). He would wind someone up until they argued back, and he would feel then that the 'debate' was going well. It seems, in Theo's case, that he was in fact, lonely.

Theo lived alone at number 95 Weatherwell Way in the village of High Pressure in Atmospheric town. He was always very grumpy and knew full well he had a reputation for being bad tempered and a 'loner'. He was quite proud of this for reasons known only unto him. In fact, the only person he seemed to have anything to do with is Lily Lightning. When they argued (or debated) you could hear them for miles. He would roar and she would flash her beautiful eyes until poor Rowena Rain had to knock on and pour down on both of them to calm them down. That's what a thunderstorm is you know! It's Theo and Lily 'debating' loudly.

A few doors down from Theo lived Sally Sunshine who owns the village teashop which is always in perfect order.

Whilst serving tea one day to Lily, Sally heard her mention that she had not seen Theo for some time as whenever she visited him lately, he seemed worse than ever and would be permanently argumentative.

He would roar at her until she got cross with him and flashed her eyes ominously.

His furniture would rattle about the house like an angry force of nature. This had, of course, put Lily off visiting him.

However, Sally could only see the good in her neighbours. She had noticed Theo's soiled net curtains and his overgrown garden, which appeared similar to the deep, dark forest that surrounds the village and the rival village of Harsh Elements. Sally felt as though he needed help. Always up for a challenge she decided to recruit her village neighbours to help raise Theo's spirits.

Sally called for a meeting to be held in her tearoom - sandwiches and cake were of course provided as she liked to do things right and proper. The meeting went on for some time as some villagers had been offended by Theo at one time or another. One person said she had bid him good morning one day and he had scowled at her and was rude. Another said she had smiled at him and was greeted by a hard stare until he turned his back on her and went into his house, slamming the door behind him. So, as you can imagine the idea of helping him was not greeted with much enthusiasm, if any. However, Lily told of a time when she caught Theo unawares, and he looked so incredibly sad that she admitted it brought tears to her eyes. So, it was concluded that something terrible must have happened to him in his past. After much persuading and cajoling, Sally managed to get some of the neighbours to agree to help and the following tasks were meted out:

Robin Rainbow, who works at the paint factory, was appointed to paint the house. Lily argued she could have that done in a flash, but Sally felt it would be nice to encourage more neighbours to be involved as a community.

Bobby Breeze was to dry the paint as quickly as possible.

Rowena Rain and Rosie Raindrop agreed to wash the windows and curtains, and Sally was to dry the washing.

Because Lily is so fast, she was asked to tend to the garden.

Shooting Star felt she could dust the furniture with her sparkling polish. Other neighbours were to be look-outs so the work could be completed whilst Theo was out of the house.

With the list of tasks completed everyone knew exactly what they had to do and couldn't wait to cheer up Theo and make his house a nicer place for him.

The biggest problem they encountered, was how to lure Theo away from his home whilst the jobs were carried out.

A plan was hatched which involved Harry Hurricane sending an invite to Theo to visit Hurricane Hall to practice his earth-shattering roar for Harry's up-coming Halloween party. Cedric Shower, who is Harry's loyal servant, was sent to deliver the invitation. He knocked at the door and Theo asked him angrily what he wanted, as he was annoyed at being disturbed. After quaking in his shoes with his knobbly knees knocking, Cedric presented him with the invitation in a gilded envelope and Theo had no option but to accept, as any invitation from the Hall was always given top priority by those invited. Theo angrily accepted the invitation and slammed the door in poor Cedric's face.

As Theo made his way to Hurricane Hall he wondered about the reason behind his invite.

"He's gone" said Sally "but we only have 90 minutes to get the task done." Well, they worked like an army of ants - scrubbing, washing, cleaning, painting, and gardening, not even leaving time for a cup of tea in the teashop.

Shooting Star polished the old wooden furniture and changed it from a dusty mess into something fit for royalty. She could even see her face in it.

Robin Rainbow made the ceiling brilliant white with blue, pink, yellow and green walls! Such lovely rainbow colours he thought. A bit dazzling thought everyone else, but cheerful. There was also an ornate mirror which was very shiny due to Shooting Star's hard work. In the back garden Billy Wind and Bobby Breeze were working away, and the curtains were no longer dusty and musty. Lily had already mowed the lawn in the front garden, planted flowers and trimmed all the hedges. She was so fast she had also built a new shed.

The result was so brilliant. It was the brightest house in the village!

With all tasks completed (and it must be noted to a very high standard indeed, as anything less would not suit Sally) the villagers hid behind various bits of furniture to surprise Theo when he returned.

They received word from the lookouts that he was on his way. They heard his footsteps on the path outside and the latch on the door as he lifted it to enter the house. They all jumped up and shouted "*surprise, surprise*" in unison.

He was indeed very surprised and rather angry to discover the changes made to his home. He was so angry that he let out an almighty roar that sent shockwaves throughout the village causing the windows to rattle in their frames, the trees to shake from their roots and the birds to fly for the safety of their nests. It frightened most of the Weather people and they left rather rapidly!

Once on his own in number 95, Theo looked around at the transformation and noticed the polished floors, the whiteness of the curtains and most of all, the shiny furniture and clean mirror in which he saw himself reflected for the first time in many years.

Thinking how nice things were and, for the first time in a long time, feeling really pleased, he said to himself, "I won't let them know I am pleased" and with a sly wink, "as I have my reputation to keep."

Little did he know that his closest neighbours were peeping at him through the lovely shiny windows, and they crept away feeling happy and contented with their achievement and knowing that, at last, they had seen Theo smile.

Chapter 2 – HALLOWEEN AT HURRICANE HALL.

Everybody loves a party and none more so than Harry Hurricane who lives in Hurricane Hall. He invited all the villagers to his annual Halloween party where there were lots of surprises and things that go bump in the night!

Harry Hurricane decided that this year his party was to be the best ever. His guests included the following:

Theo Thunder for his fabulous roaring qualities;

Lily Lightning who could brighten up any room she was in;

Darren Drizzle, Billy Wind, Rowena Rain and Rosie Raindrop to clear the deep, dark forest

once Freddie Fog and Monica Mist had done their best at being mysterious;
Shooting Star to pretend she was a firework;
Clara and Claudia Cloud to dish out drinks to the guests;
Lord and Lady Mayoress Sky and Mother Nature were, of course, VIP's;
The staff consisted of Cedric Shower (who is Harry's devoted and loyal servant);
Monica Mist who cleans for Harry Hurricane and for Freddie Fog. Freddie resides at Foggy Fort and is secretly a jealous rival of Harry Hurricane.
Mr. Moon volunteered to be the Events Co-Ordinator.
Sally Sunshine took charge of all the catering in her usual efficient way;
Theo (after roaring) and Lily (after startling everyone with her flashing eyes) together with Shooting Star, were all delegated to take charge of the fabulous firework display;
Darren Drizzle had the added task of DJ;
Jack Frost (in cahoots with Ivor Ice) caused the surface to be icy and slippery.

The costumes worn by Freddie Fog and Monica Mist were made so as to blend easily with the deep, dark forest.

Mr. Moon was rushed off his feet with all the organising he had to do. He didn't wear a costume as the invitation asked him to do, but formal attire. He felt he was much too important for that (or so he believed).

Sally had a very calming influence with her soothing smile. She had provided a wide selection of food which included toffee apples, Parkin cake, jacket potatoes - with a glorious selection of fillings: candy floss as light as air, popcorn, popping candy, which burst in the mouth and made one giggle, hot dogs, and apples for bobbing. A cauldron of fruit punch was also made which was stirred by Clara and Claudia Cloud who were dressed as witches.

Pumpkins were made into Jack O'Lanterns, which were well lit by Sally and spread amongst the trees in the deep, dark forest and the hall.

There were black spiders as big as Harry Hurricane's hand, all spinning ultra large cobwebs upon the walls and ceilings. Bats circled the proceedings.

All guests were to be met at the entrance to the hall by Harry Hurricane himself who was dressed as Count Dracula, accompanied by Cedric who was dressed as Igor, right down to a bright yellow pair of tights on his legs and a pillow stuffed up his jumper to give him a humpback.

Freddie and Monica hatched a plan to ruin the party as Freddie was very jealous of the wonderful spread of food and popularity of Harry Hurricane. They decided they would ruin the party and blame it on the legend of the ghost said to reside in the hall, who was rumoured to be an old chef and whose name was Sirocco. They arranged for the food to be substituted by Freddie's henchmen by providing snails in a mud pie, worm cake, sour milk for the punch drink, apples rotten with maggots, shriveled turnips, and black beetles in the popcorn.

Before the party there were to be events outside which included a treasure hunt in the deep, dark forest. The deep, dark forest was a very scary, murky place indeed. Rumour had it that there were large cats who hid in the trees and all you could see of them were their glowing eyes. Spiders were huge and spun enormous, sticky webs throughout the trees whilst vampire bats circled in the sky above looking for prey below. Rats and mice foraged in the undergrowth where snakes lurked under the trees ready to pounce and there was always an owl hooting away eerily.

Mr. Moon would often pass over and hope to shed some light on the forest but there were wolves prowling about and as soon as they spied him, they would howl ferociously, and he would slide away and hide behind a member of the cloud family. Folklore told of a young person who entered the forest and came out looking like a wizened old person with snow white hair. So, you see reader, nobody would go in there alone.

Well, would you?

The guests were led into the deep, dark forest for the treasure hunt.

There was lots of back slapping camaraderie, but they were quite frightened.

At least they entered as a group - safety in numbers and all that!

In the deep, dark forest Freddie and Monica were busy swirling around and making the forest denser, causing confusion and panic amongst the guests, in a bid to distract from the ongoing treachery at the hall. They made the branches of the trees sway like a hundred menacing arms in the dark. The leaves were flying about as if they were desperate to escape from the confusion and the hard October soil turned to mud.

The guests were beaten back and swirled around and knocked off their feet as Billy Wind and Rowena Rain worked together to clear the thick dense fog. Billy blew so hard, and Rowena poured down so heavily that the trees bent over in fright. Rosie Raindrop did her best to help. Bats were flying about causing mayhem and the guests felt their hair stand on end as they fell about in the deluge. Eventually the fog and mist cleared, and the guests ran in fright back to the hall, forgetting all about their treasure hunt. Back to safety - or so they thought!

To the embarrassment of Harry Hurricane, when the guests returned to the hall the food was found to be rotten. Cedric believed this to be the work of the ghost and was so scared he became hysterical and upset. His hump wobbled like jelly in an earthquake and his knees knocked together!

Monica found it all quite amusing and was sat in the corner cackling and chortling away like a witch. The rats and mice were having a field day running amok.

"Oh no" exclaimed Cedric with a tremor in his voice, "it's the ghost of Sirocco, a chef who used to work here at Hurricane Hall many years ago."

(So named Sirocco, after the famous, hot wind that blows on Earth from North Africa), was a big, big man, with dark mean eyes and eyebrows like two thick sweeping brushes. His temper was so bad that when he bellowed his hairy nostrils flared and his mouth opened like a deep, dark cavern. His voice could be heard throughout the hall and beyond.

His rages caused mayhem amongst the underlings in his kitchen and the timid scullery maid was often found trembling as she hid in the pantry, or under the stairs or, in fact, anywhere to get away from his terrible temper.

Billy knew all about him. Oh yes, he knew alright. He had heard the family talk. (After all, Sirocco was his great grandfather!)

"Sirocco never liked strangers cooking in his kitchen", continued Cedric, "and that is why he's turned all the lovely party food rotten and stinky. He haunts Hurricane Hall and will never leave this place", and, with that, Cedric sat with a plop on to the stone floor and began to suck on his thumb.

Harry Hurricane tried his best to reassure his frightened, little minion, Cedric, that the stories about Sirocco the chef were just that, silly stories. Cedric though, on the other hand, was not convinced. "And quite rightly so" thought Billy.

Darren Drizzle, who was dressed in a suit of armour as his contribution to fancy dress, was invisible to the henchmen and, whilst setting up his DJ equipment and playlist, saw all the events unfold. He told Mr. Moon who then accused the henchmen. They, of course, denied this and said it must have been the ghost.

Mr. Moon used his magical moonbeams from his eyes and was able to see all, which caused Freddie and Monica to confess to their dastardly deeds and plans to spoil the party.

Punishment was meted out and Freddie and Monica were put into the stocks and pelted with rotten food. They were then banished from the hall and sloped off, together with their henchmen into the night.

Back at Hurricane Hall, Shooting Star, being magical, sprinkled her magic stardust over the hall and the food and celebrations were returned to their former glory. The result being that the festivities carried on well into the night and a good time was had by all.

High up in the attic and laughing to himself at all the crazy antics of the party, the Hurricane Hall ghost was waiting for midnight - the bewitching hour!

Chapter 3 - THE REVENGE OF FREDDIE FOG

Freddie Fog was angry and felt humiliated after what had happened at the Halloween party at Hurricane Hall. He hatched a plan to get revenge on Harry Hurricane after Freddie's plans to spoil his Halloween party were scuppered. After some thought he decided that it was *all* the fault of the Weather People who, he felt, humiliated him, throwing all the rotten food at them whilst in the stocks. Monica Mist then piped up, "I'm a big fan of getting my five a day of fruit and veg, but not when it's mushy and half of it goes up my nose."

Freddie Fog decided to call upon an old friend - Dame Ava Avalanche. She was a nasty old woman, cold and bitter and scared everyone including Freddie Fog. She had cold bright blue eyes, icy cold spindly fingers and breath that freezes anyone who encountered it. Freddie Fog called on her to help with his revenge plan.

Freddie sent Monica Mist to Alaska as this is where Dame Ava Avalanche lived in an ice palace near to the home of Sir Gregory Glacier.

"Eeeh", exclaimed Monica Mist, "If I've got to go and see her, I'd better change my frock and put my false teeth in, because she's a posh and titled lady." Off went Monica Mist on her quest to return to Weatherwell Way with Dame Ava Avalanche, who agreed to Freddie's plan and arrived with great majesty and importance, while Monica Mist trailed behind her. She travelled in a carriage which was crystal clear and made entirely of ice. It was pulled by six snarling, Husky dogs.

As her carriage crossed the drawbridge of Foggy Fort, the flowing water of the moat below turned to ice thick enough to skate on.

Freddie Fog and Dame Ava Avalanche had strategic talks to plan their maneuvers and it was agreed to turn Weatherwell Way and Atmospheric Town into an eternal winter and to take over Hurricane Hall where they could reign supreme over all they surveyed. It was decided to hypnotise all the villagers and to lure them into the deep, dark forest near High Pressure Village. There they would be frozen in time and imprisoned forever in a snow globe the size of a mountain.

Dame Ava Avalanche climbed up onto the turrets of Foggy Fort and, looking down upon the village, cast her evil, icy glare across the land below.

All the Weather people were stopped in their tracks as her evil spell was cast and took hold of them. They were then enticed into the deep, dark forest and the evil deed was completed.

With a final ear-splitting cackle, Dame Ava Avalanche waved her icy staff across the forest and sealed the Weather People into the snow globe. How would they ever escape now?

It was Christmas Eve in Weatherwell Way and Jack Frost and his best pal Stuart (Stuey) Sunbeam were playing snueling (snow/dueling). A game where Jack Frost threw icicles or snowballs at Stuey from different angles and at different heights. Stuey had to hit and melt them. If he hit them, he got a point, if he missed Jack Frost got the point. One of the snowballs hit Stuey in the face and knocked him onto his back. The snowball was so hard, like a stone.

"Steady on mate!" shouted Stuey, "There is no need to throw them at me with such force, and that was extra cold too." Jack Frost was a bit bemused as he didn't throw it that hard and even he was shivering with the cold. It certainly was getting colder by the minute, even the chest of Robin Redbreast had turned white.

The only place that seemed to have some warmth was Sally Sunshine's tearoom. Spying on them from afar, Dame Ava Avalanche questioned how they had not been affected by her hypnotic spell and neither had Sally, working away in her tearoom.

Dame Ave Avalanche decided to visit the tearoom to find out why Sally was still not hypnotised. She instructed Monica Mist to capture Jack Frost and Stuey and take them to Hurricane Hall.

"Take my Husky dogs with you for protection" she barked "And I shall visit the tearoom."

Monica Mist, sitting on the back of one of the Husky dogs, wearing a tiara made of pure ice, approached Jack Frost and Stuey, who couldn't believe their eyes, and both fell about laughing at the sight before them.

"Stop this laughing at once. If you knew what I know you would have more respect. So be very careful. You know nothing of what is happening."

They asked her, "Why, what is happening?" and she replied, "What is happening you nincompoops?! My mistress has arrived to reign over the whole land. You will now come with me to my mistress, and she will put you in a trance when you can then join your friends in the snow globe in the deep, dark forest." As the snarling dogs bared their sharp teeth and growled threateningly, Jack Frost whispered to Stuey to play along with the plot and Stuey gave his pal a knowing nod and wink.

On arrival at the hall Jack Frost and Stuey found that Sally was a imprisoned by Dame Ava Avalanche and was being held as a captive in the dungeons.

Pretending to be under the spell of Dame Ava Avalanche the boys planned to free Sally. You may wonder, reader, why they could not be hypnotised? Well, you see, Jack was made of frost which means snow had no effect on him and Stuey was too hot. However, they played along so that they could save Sally and the Weather people.

Monica Mist was the guard on duty in the dungeon. She loved her job now that she was the top person in charge and liked nothing better than to jingle her keys to show her importance. Jack Frost and Stuey pretended to be hypnotised and acted as minions. They brought some food and drink down to Monica Mist. The drink that they brought down to her seemed to 'accidentally' fall from the tray. How convenient is that? This made a puddle on the floor which Jack Frost immediately froze. This then caused Monica Mist to slip all over the floor and land with a bump on the bars of the cell where Sally was being held. As quick as Lily Lightning would have done, Sally grabbed the keys from the belt around the waist of Monica Mist and opened the door. Looking Monica Mist in the eye, Sally then grabbed her and threw her into the cell and locked the door. She then threw in Monica Mist's false teeth and tiara, and they all escaped.

Dame Ava Avalanche could not understand why, when confronted by Jack Frost, Stuey, and Sally, that they were not under her spell.

"Easy" exclaimed Jack Frost, "Ice on ice - no dice and Stuey and Sally are too hot to handle."

"Now" said Sally, "It's time to bring you down to size." With the combined power of Sally and Stuey, they blasted Dame Ava Avalanche and reduced her to a snowball the size of a pebble. (How about that for global warming!)

The spell was now broken, as was the snow globe and all the villagers were free to go back to their homes to celebrate Christmas.

In the distance they could hear the sound of jingle bells and knew that Father Christmas was near. They gave Dame Ava Avalanche into the hands of Father Christmas, who put her into a magic box and took her back to Alaska and handed her to Sir Gregory Glacier where, now being a snowball, she could do no harm.

And what about Freddie Fog? Well, his plans once more were well and truly scuppered. But he knew one day he would get his own back - just you see if he didn't!

He went to bed in a miserable sulk and missed out on all the lovely Christmas Eve festivities whilst Monica Mist languished in her dungeon. Unfortunately, that's what happens when you are mean to others.

Meanwhile, the villagers all returned to their homes and later congregated at Sally Sunshine's tearoom for mince pies and hot milk. Sally had, of course, as was her way, decorated the room and had an extra-large Christmas tree which was beautifully decorated. How lovely to be with special friends on such a lovely occasion. They laughed and danced into the night and wished all a very happy Christmas.

CHAPTER 4: BUNFIGHT AT WEATHERWELL WAY

Lily Lightning was an athlete and sports woman. She had many awards and trophies to her name that she had won for her many races and sporting achievements over the years.

She started each day with a morning run around Weatherwell Way which consisted of running on the outskirts of The Deep Dark Forest and up to Beacon Hill, locally known as 'the backies'. One particular day she was wearing one of her many outfits. This one was made up of pink Lycra shorts, sparkly black crop top, snazzy trainers with lightning stripes and her lightning bolt earrings. With her hair in a high ponytail and her fit-bit watch, she was ready to go.

On her way down to begin her jog she met Sonia Squirrel who was feeling out of breath and looking rather exhausted.

"Oh dear", panted Sonia "I feel so out of shape after all the nuts I've stored up throughout the Winter and, after all the food I've over-indulged in over Christmas. I wish 1 was as fit and energetic as you Lily! I need to lose some weight if I'm going to fit into my swimsuit in time for the holiday in Heatwave City."

"Anyway," she continued "I'm off now to Sally Sunshine's Tearoom for a coffee and a bun!"

Lily had always had an ambition to set up a gymnasium and health food shop selling healthy shakes, healthy food, and energy bars. Sonia Squirrel had given Lily an idea.

On her way down from the 'backies', Lily met Theo Thunder who was going to Sally Sunshine's tearoom because, after the hard work that everyone had put into tidying up his house and making it nice, he thought that he should make more of an effort with the rest of the Weather people and be more sociable.

Inspired by her new thought of setting up a gym, Lily thought the only problem was that she didn't have the space for it all in her house.

She decided to go with Theo to Sally Sunshine's tearoom and see if Sally would let her put some of her health food and shakes onto her tearoom menu. When asked, Sally got uppity and flatly refused saying, "This is a traditional tearoom and there is no place for your sort of nutty buffet on my menu and in my tearoom. I suggest you take your ideas elsewhere!"

Not to be downhearted or defeated, Lily turned heel on her lightning bolt snazzy trainers, her eyes flashing with anger and determination.

She said to herself "I'll show you Sally Sunshine - just watch this space."

In her kitchen at number 94, Weatherwell Way, Lily set about shaking and baking and within two minutes (because she was exceptionally fast) her healthy shakes and nutty cakes, energy bars and tofu squares were ready for sale.

The next day Sally rose as usual at the crack of dawn to set up the tearoom. She drew back the curtains and behold, what did she see but Lily across the road from her tearoom, with a stall nicely filled with healthy goodies. Without even stopping to put the tea urn on or beat an egg, she stormed over to Lily and her golden-brown eyes turned the colour of black cinders as she was so furious.

Her normal neat and tidy, corn coloured hair stood on end and was pure red with anger.

Sally challenged Lily saying, "Excuse me, what do you think you are doing. You are taking away my livelihood by enticing my customers to your ridiculous selection of 'rabbit food'."

Lily retorted "How dare you say my products are 'rabbit food'. They are extremely healthy unlike your cakes and buns."

Their voices getting louder and louder in confrontation awoke all the residents in Weatherwell Way. "What's going on ladies" said Eddie Eclipse.

He could see that Sally was visibly upset and wrapping his calming arms around her shaking shoulders, he led her quietly up the path to her tearoom. He returned to try and calm Lily, but she was inconsolable. As he was having no success in solving the disagreement, he felt that Mother Nature being the supreme force, should be called upon to intervene.

With this in mind, he went to see Mother Nature where she lived in Cascading Falls Chateau and explained all the commotion between Sally and Lily.

"Oh, dear me" exhaled Mother Nature, "We cannot have this. It is not good. We must nip this in the bud." She asked Eddie Eclipse to escort Sally and Lily to her chateau so that she could mediate between them and work out this problem satisfactorily.

Sally was the first to be escorted by Eddie Eclipse to see Mother Nature. On her arrival Sally was offered a calming goblet of nectar by Mother Nature's manservant, Darren Drizzle.

She was shown to the study where she was asked to wait until Lily was brought in.

Eddie Eclipse returned to Weatherwell Way to collect Lily. The villagers were all agog and excited about the events that had taken place that morning. What would be the outcome they wondered?

Back at the chateau, Lily was also offered a drink by Darren Drizzle and was then shown to the study where Mother Nature and Sally sat.

After long discussions and much deliberation, a resolution was reached. Mother Nature, using her wisdom and guidance, commented that, "The solution is staring us all in the face." Looking Sally in the eyes she said, "Whenever I have been down to your tearoom, I have been impressed by the community spirit which exists in your establishment - your souffles, by the way are divine and I would like to place a regular order for some of your souffles to be delivered for my committee meeting, which is held each month." This made Sally glow with pride.

"As for you Lily, I am prepared to offer you my conservatory in which you could have your gym and health food shop. Hopefully, this will resolve your problems and we can, once again, return to our harmonious and peaceful friendships."

Both ladies agreed that this was a wonderful solution and shook hands. They then left the chateau arm in arm, giggling all the way back to the village. Sally announced to the villagers that the problems were now over and invited everyone back to her tearoom making Lily her special guest.

Chapter 5 - THEFT FROM CASCADING FALLS CHATEAU

At 2.00 pm precisely on the 11th day of each month, Mother Nature held a meeting for the Heads of Committees of various charities. The meetings were always held in her beautiful drawing room. She was always exquisitely dressed as she liked beauty to be all around her, within her surroundings and beyond. Hence, Rowena Rain really worked hard to keep the grass and flowers well-watered, and Shooting Star was always brightening the inside of the house. Mother Nature was a tad annoyed at the humans on Earth for the problems concerning the Ozone Layer... but that's another story.

Her footman, Darren Drizzle, a man of many talents and completely loyal to Mother Nature, always welcomed the members and announced their presence as each one arrives.

The first to arrive was always Cecelia Cuckoo, who liked to be very early as she always took the minutes of the meeting. She was always very precise and liked everything to be in order. She was so organised that she even lay her eggs in some other bird's nest so that she did not have her home disrupted by little ones and to keep them out of the way of her husband, Clive Cuckoo, who today, was helping in the kitchen. He was an idle layabout and normally only did things for others when it was profitable for him. Nobody knows this fact though as Cecelia was an extremely private person and kept lots of things to herself.

Next to arrive for this meeting was Lord and Lady Sky who are very old friends of Mother Nature. Lord Sky retired to the library whilst Lady Sky joined her friend in the drawing room just to oversee the proceedings.

Catherine Wheel from the Firework family together with Muriel Moon, who oversee the light entertainment for various functions, arrived with Winifred Wheat, who was Head of the Festival Charity Committee.

Harry Hurricane was allowed to join Lord Sky in the library, as he had loaned Cedric Shower out to help Monice Mist with handing out refreshments after the meeting. Mr. Moon was also there and had made his way to the library to join the menfolk.

Last to arrive was Molly Magpie whose charity was the Bird Sanctuary. She made a grand entrance dressed in a beautiful cape of blue/black and white and her hair was cut in a feathered style and was blue/black, the same colour as her cape.

Sally Sunshine appeared at the door. She had brought her delicious souffles for Mother Nature who adored them and usually ate the lot herself.

As Sally left, she encountered Lily Lightning. The two of them had become good friends since the bun fight and loved a little chat. Lily had just finished a session in her gym which she held in the conservatory of the chateau. Sally remarked how beautiful Mother Nature always was with her exquisite clothes and her wonderful jewelry. "Some of that jewelry is so lovely, especially the ruby necklace" remarked Lily. "It certainly is" agreed Sally.

Darren Drizzle overheard their conversation and agreed with them. He had been entrusted with the key to Mother Nature's safe as she had not had time to hide this away safely. He felt very honoured that she would trust him so. However, reader, Darren Drizzle was not the only one to overhear that particular conversation!

The meeting progressed and as usual, ended amicably.

Members were invited to congregate in the huge dining hall where they mingled and were offered canapes and drinks by Monica and Cedric who, for a change, were on their best behaviour.

Mother Nature decided that she would like to freshen up and retired to her boudoir.

Suddenly the guests heard a shrill scream. It was positively blood curdling. Lord Sky took the stairs two at a time and was shocked at the sight before his eyes.

Mother Nature's room was thoroughly trashed and the safe lay wide open with the key in the door. All her jewelry was gone, including the famous ruby necklace. She had fainted and was lay on the floor.

Lord Sky managed to revive Mother Nature and she trembled as she asked, "Who could have done this?!" Everyone was all agog. It was a terrible time. Some even accused Lily because she was always so quick, and the room seem to have been ransacked in no time. Lily was most offended and resolved then and there not to speak to anyone ever again, except for Sally, her new BFF (best friends forever).

Darren Drizzle phoned for the police to come at once to try and solve the mystery. He calmed Mother Nature down and ordered all the guests to congregate in the library and locked the door so no-one could leave. He realised that whoever the thief was, that they were also a pick pocket as the key had been taken from the back pocket of his trousers.

What a state of affairs!

Monica was clearing the food away and heard that there was a thief in the chateau. She went into a dizzy panic and Cedric couldn't understand what she was babbling on about.

"It's me" she cried "I'm the one, I took it!" She then collapsed onto the floor and was hysterical. Poor Cedric didn't quite know what to do.

There was a knock at the door and Darren Drizzle went to see who was there.

In came Inspector Angela Air who was renowned for getting results. She had succeeded in putting Dolly Damp into prison after she had admitted to theft and burglary! Proving that she was talented at her job.

Inspector Air was accompanied by her sidekick Detective Jason Jetstream who was always nibbling a carrot. (He was in awe of her and terrified of her at the same time.)

"Ok, what's going on here then?" Inspector Air demanded to know. She then noticed Monica crawling round the floor looking scared and very guilty.

"Are you the one?" asked Inspector Air. "Come on - own up. If you confess the judge may be lenient with you." Monica was beside herself. She stuttered and stammered out "I don't believe that they have sent for you, such a famous Police Inspector, just because I was tempted to take a souffle when no-one was looking."

"Oh, for goodness sake" muttered Inspector Air under her breath "Get up Monica. Have you not been told that it is the famous ruby necklace that has been stolen?" Monica was so relieved she dissolved into another fit of crying and had to be carried out to lie down somewhere.

Detective Jetstream was busy checking the outside of the building as he had noticed the bedroom window was wide open, meaning that he felt the thief had escaped that way.

"My, he's improving," thought Inspector Air, "He's actually showing signs of having a brain." She could be quite harsh sometimes, but she always got results.

"Did you find anything Jason?" she asked.

"Actually," he replied as he chewed nervously on his carrot, "I found a feather just on the ground below the bedroom window." Such an important clue was not overlooked by Inspector Air, and she said that all the guests were to remain in the library until her investigation was over.

Meanwhile, in the library, speculation and looks of accusation were rife. The atmosphere was beginning to turn hostile. I kid you not reader, mayhem and chaos reigned.

Who do you think the thief was reader? Who do you think overheard Sally Sunshine and Lily Lightning talking?

Could it have been Lily? No, surely not, she was in the chateau alone on many occasions running her gym and if it had been her, she risked losing her livelihood. Could it have been Sally? After all she had been overheard discussing the necklace with Lily earlier. No, surely not. It was well known that she was comfortably off and was never seen dressed up but always in her pinafore doing her baking, so why would she want the necklace.

Could it have been Darren Drizzle? No - surely not. He adored Mother Nature. Well, it was speculated that he more than adored her but had to be satisfied to worship her from afar. On and on it went. Who was to blame?

Surely not Cecelia Cuckoo who, after all, was a dark horse. Anyway, it couldn't be her as she had been seen copying up her notes and had not moved, even to join in the buffet. Mother Nature was terribly upset to see her people so angry and suspicious. Even though she loved beautiful things, it wasn't worth all this.

After about half an hour, Inspector Air entered the library and looking straight at Molly Magpie he accused her of the theft. Shock horror! Molly, of course, denied this and demanded that Inspector Air prove her accusation.

"Of course, it was you" stated Inspector Air scathingly "Because the feather found outside the window was yours and you have one missing from your cape. Also, your fingerprints were on the key in the safe door. (A lie, but Inspector Air was tricking Molly for a confession) "That could have been a feather from any other bird" scoffed Molly, "And anyway, I wore gloves."

"So, it was you" said Inspector Air triumphantly. "Now then, where is the necklace and other jewelry Molly?"

Molly had no option now but to confess all. She said she had flown out of the window and passed the jewelry to Clive Cuckoo who was going to sell it on, and they would then divide the money. She thought if she was going to prison, she wasn't going to take the whole blame.

"Now then, where is the necklace and other jewelry Clive Cuckoo?" demanded Inspector Air. On hearing this, Clive attempted to get away, but Inspector Air had seen this coming and with her magic air powers she had blown the door firmly shut. Detective Jetstream then sat on him and handcuffed him.

The mystery was solved when Clive confessed that he had hidden the ruby necklace in the strawberry jelly so it wouldn't be noticed. The other jewelry was stashed in a souffle.

Good job Monica didn't know that, or she would have been beside herself if she had bitten into the jewelry!

One has to have some sympathy with Cecelia Cuckoo. After all, it was her husband who was guilty. She resigned her post then and there and, feeling totally embarrassed, left with a red face which almost matched the colour of the stolen necklace!

Clive Cuckoo was taken off to prison with Molly Magpie and guess what reader, as they were entering the prison, which is called Twilight Towers, Dolly Damp was leaving. She had served her sentence. Oh aye - she had indeed. She would not forget and someday she would get her own back.

"Inspector Air will get her comeuppance just you wait and see," she muttered to herself as she made her way to the infamous Foggy Fort.

Well reader, Dolly Damp and her escapades is another story, isn't it? Meanwhile, Molly Magpie and Clive Cuckoo languish in prison doing their 'bird' as it's known in the criminal world. Well, they do say birds of a feather, flock together.

Chapter 6 – HOLIDAY IN HEATWAVE CITY

Christmas had come and gone. Don't you find reader that after all the festivities, unless you have a special event coming up, things seem to be a bit flat. And so, at this time of the year, the Weather People usually took a holiday to liven things up for themselves.

They met together in Sally Sunshine's tearoom to discuss where they wanted to go this year. "I know" said Sally, "We could all go to Heatwave City where there are lots of things going on."

"What a good idea!" agreed Stuey Sunbeam.

"We could enter our band for the annual talent contest which takes place about now."

The band in question consisted of Theo Thunder on drums, obviously, because he just loved to bang and crash about, which he did to his heart's content. Bobby Breeze and Billy Wind played the guitars and Rosie Raindrop tinkled away on the keyboard. The backing group for the lead singer was Claude and Clara Cloud. The lead singer being Tallulah Tornado who has a voice so loud she can shatter glass. She is a very flamboyant character and was also aching to take part in the dance competition, so she was up for the idea of going to Heatwave City. There she would meet up with her dance partner Eric Earthquake, another flamboyant character.

In Heatwave City there was a dance club adjoining Climate Beach. This is where Sue Narmi and her partner Chris Cyclone would hang out. Chris Cyclone secretly loved Tallulah Tornado and Eric Earthquake was his biggest rival. Sue Narmi had no time at all for Tallulah Tornado. This all meant that the competition was taken very seriously indeed.

So seriously, that the judges felt perhaps it may be wiser to give every one of the dancers scores of 10 to avoid any confrontations. Oh dear, how fraught was this going to be?

The band, however, and the rest of the Weather People were oblivious to the goings on of the dancers and were really looking forward to their holiday. Well, who wouldn't!

They were met at their chosen hotel by Sue Narmi and Chris Cyclone and given a run-down of the various activities they could take part in, which of course, included the competition. After freshening up and changing into their swimwear they all met together on the beach. Monica Mist felt this was a good opportunity to practice her act with Cedric

Shower. After their magic tricks (which were surprisingly good) they decided to have a go at their acrobatics.

Their acrobatics didn't go as well as their magic tricks, but they both felt it would be alright on the night.

"I can't wait to take that trophy home" remarked Monica confidently. She, of course, meant to her home and not to Cedric's place. No way was she going to share it with him. Poor Cedric!

Rosie Raindrop was so excited and was sat thinking about the type of makeup she would use. She was anxious to get back to the hotel to try it out. She said the same to Monica who thought to herself, "Well I don't need any makeup, as my natural beauty is enough to light up any stage, even more so than Sally Sunshine ever could." Cedric was feeling restless as he needed to get back to rinse out his white lycra tights. He told Monica he must get back to do this and she said, "Well, I need to relax before tonight's performance, so I am going to hitch a lift back to the hotel on a donkey."

In time they all drifted back to their hotel to change into their costumes for their various acts. The compere for the evening was Solomon Sandstorm who looked magnificent in his red sequined jacket, bow tie, white trousers, and a sparkling white showbiz smile to match. Sally Sunshine was wearing a designer gown in blue which shimmered in the lights and her hair was piled up in a creation beyond imagination. She had a lovely voice and was to sing an aria from the opera Madame Butterfly. In the dance section Tallulah Tornado and Eric Earthquake decided to dance the Paso Dobli and Sue Narmi and Chris Cyclone entered for the Argentine Tango.

The Band looked fabulous in their glittery outfits and last, but not least, Nina Northwind was to appear dressed in a baby doll pink dress with a lollipop and her hair done up in golden ringlets as she sang a song from the movies. All in all, there was a full program of events to look forward to.

However, there had been a problem with the judges, as one had fallen ill. Lily Lightning stepped in to make up the panel of four people. The other three were Boris Balmy, Robin Rainbow and Marion Monsoon. Marion saw this as an opportunity to regain her fame as she was once a glamorous movie star. Lily was very keen to keep to the rules and they were read out before the competition, one of the rules being that no judge should be related to any of the acts.

Well, the time had come - the suspense was over. With a drum roll from the band, Solomon stepped up on to the stage and suddenly the spotlight was upon him. He looked grand as he announced, "I am pleased and honoured to welcome you ladies, gentlemen and children, to this year's competition for up-and-coming new talent. The first act will be a young band called 'Storm' who originate from Weatherwell Way. Please give them a round of applause."

The band played and sang rock and roll and Tallulah Tornado, as good as her name, nearly shattered all the lights in the theatre. After riotous applause the band were followed by Sally Sunshine singing her aria and she was, or course, superb.

Next appeared Monica Mist and Cedric Shower, who really were a sight to behold. Their magic tricks were good, but their acrobatics left a lot to be desired. Cedric lay down on his back with his legs in the air, and Monica took a flying leap across the room to try to land on her stomach on the top of his feet... it didn't work! Well reader, did we really expect it to? They both dropped into a heap on the floor. However, the audience thought they were clowning around and loved it. Monica whispered to Cedric "I feel we are definitely in with a chance here, listen to the applause, they love me... erm us."

Before the dance acts, Nina Northwind tap danced onto the stage singing her song. It has to be said that she sang very sweetly, and the audience couldn't tell from a distance that she was in fact 30 years old. She really was quite something.

Finally, the dancers came on to show their skills. Both performed magnificently and it was all rather dramatic to say the least. Not a foot out of place. Whilst the judges totted up their points the audience were treated to a performance from the winner of the competition from the last year then there was an interval.

There was a fanfare whilst Solomon returned to the stage with the results in his hand. The suspense was intense. After a long pause he announced the first place "And the winner of this year's competition is... Nina Northwind!"

The others couldn't believe it but applauded all the same. She went up to receive her trophy from the judges and was overheard saying "Oh thank you so much Auntie Marion." Shock horror! Even some of the audience heard this but no one more than Lily Lightning. As quick as her name she disqualified Nina who ran from the stage sobbing with a red-faced Marion Monsoon following behind. She was furious. Gone now was her chance of regaining her fame.

Monica and Cedric were asked to perform once more whilst the judges huddled together again to do a recount of the points. Solomon then took his place on stage yet again. The results were announced and this time Tallulah (who remember had also performed in the band) and Eric were the winners - much to the chagrin of Sue Narmi and her partner who came second, but she let them know in no uncertain terms as she was heard muttering, "Just you all wait until next year - we will sweep the lot of you away". Sally Sunshine came third and was thrilled and she couldn't wait to display her trophy in her tearoom for all to see. The band came fourth, but they were happy about that.

Monica and Cedric were given a prize because they had stepped in at the end in good faith to help keep the audience occupied.

Monica, although she didn't win, was delighted to be recognised and poor Cedric was told by her that the award would be kept in her home until next year. Oh, dearie me! He wasn't bothered really because he had enjoyed watching Monica fall off a donkey on the beach earlier.

After a couple more days on the beach they all went home and agreed that a good time was had by all. They agreed that they would definitely return next year to compete, even after what Sue Narmi had threatened!